Curiouser and Curiouser

Pool of Tears

Book One

Written by Erin Pyne
Illustrated by Cayce Moyer

Curiouser and Curiouser: Pool of Tears, Book One, 2011
Published by Rowan Tree Books.
10652 Windsor Ct Orlando Fl, 32821

ISBN: 978-0615529127

rologue:

"No room!" The man with the large hat exclaimed. Alice stared at Hatter who held a cup of tea in each hand and was attempting to pour a third with a tea pot shoved under his elbow.

"No room! Private party!" The March Hare howled as he used one of his long fuzzy ears to wipe cake crumbs off a small plate.

"I don't mean to intrude, but…" Alice began.

"If you don't mean to, don't do it!" The March Hare cried. "But you already have intruded in a meaningless way."

"Then it is not worth mentioning." Hatter said briskly. "Clean cup!" He moved down several chairs to a large purple armchair.

"I am not here to drink your tea. I simply have a message for Hatter," Alice said stepping over several broken teacups.

"A message for me?" Hatter looked up interested. "Who from?"

"From me," she said. "So that you'll know… for the future… Do not come for me. The Red Queen is not who she claims to be. The Rabbit's Watch may be able to break Time's curse, but the Red Queen will trade you to the Queen of Hearts." Alice's eyes filled with tears.

"I… watched you die."

Hatter stared at her, the light in his eyes growing. "How do you know anything about me? Who are you?"

"I'm Alice." She stepped up to the chair Hatter was sitting in and whispered in his ear. "And you mean more to me than you'll ever know."

Chapter One: A Walk Through the Woods

Alice hurried through the streets of Oxford, her eyes searching every dark corner. Late to visit her sister, she rushed through the winding paths, worried that her friend would be lost to her forever.

She had wandered these side streets many times before. The intricate architecture, cobblestone streets, and unique history awakened her imagination to romantic stories of lovers, ghosts, and starry-eyed writers. Every distinctive door or garden gate could be an entrance to a hidden world of magical creatures and adventures.

Only Alice did not have much time to dream anymore. She was in Oxford to care for her dying sister. Suffering a broken back and head trauma after a car crash, her older sister, Lorina, had slipped into a coma at John Radcliffe Hospital. Lorina was Alice's only family; raised in foster homes and boarding schools, they had no parents to care for them. For the past two weeks, Alice had visited her sister every day, hoping that she might wake up again.

This evening, she was late. Instead of visiting her sister, she was desperately searching for a missing friend. Uncaring that her hair was wildly disheveled, or that her face was lined with worry, or that her blue eyes were watery from tears, she walked past Alice's Shop, the tourist attraction based on the Lewis Carroll books, and entered Café Loco, a tea shop and café. She quickly approached the front counter.

"Have you seen this cat?" Alice desperately asked the young man tending the shop.

"A cat?" The young man looked up as he answered. He reached up and pulled his hat back revealing dark green eyes. She held up a hastily written flyer with a photocopied picture of her brown tabby cat under the words, MISSING. "Her name is Dynamite. Dyna. She ran off this afternoon and hasn't returned!"

"Hmm," the young man put down his tea and looked at the picture shaking his head.

"Haven't seen her. You want me to hang that in the window?"

"Yes, please. That would be very kind, Mr…"

"Carter." He took the flyer and his fingers brushed Alice's hand. As he touched her, she felt a shock, like static electricity only the feeling lingered a second longer. Carter looked up sharply and said, "You shocked me!"

"No, you shocked **me**!" Alice said with a smile.

Before Alice could blink, Carter was over the counter and standing before her. He removed his hat to reveal a shock of messy black hair. He ran his fingers through his hair attempting to smooth it before replacing his hat.

"You know, now that think about it, I believe I have seen your cat. This afternoon 'round Addisons'. I can help you find her." Carter said. "It's almost closing time anyway. OY!" He shouted to the other employees in the shop.

"I'm leaving early… someone take over, eh?" Carter took a last sip of his tea and grabbed a leather satchel from behind the counter. He looked around and softly said, "I might actually miss this place."

Alice frowned at him, "You don't have to bother this much. Don't get in trouble. I'll be fine."

"Nonsense!" Carter cried, his voice squeaking slightly. "I'm great at finding cats. Dynamite can't be far; Oxford is a small town. Let's go!"

Without looking both ways, he walked directly across St. Aldates street and turned at the gates leading into Christ Church Cathedral.

Alice sighed in frustration and waited for the roads to clear before crossing. Carter led the way, past the tourists exiting the huge cathedral, and onto the dirt path leading behind the Oxford colleges. Alice followed holding her flyers close to her chest.

"Where did you say you saw her?" She asked hurrying to catch up.

"In the woods," Carter replied. "I was walking along the path at lunch and saw your cat in the ivy. I'm sure she's still there. That's where I would be if I were a cat." He glanced back at Alice. "So, how did you lose her?"

"I… had an appointment, but I was so tired I sat down for only a second, and then I must have fallen asleep! I woke up and noticed the front door was open and Dyna had gone. Thank you for helping, by the way. It means more to me than you know."

Carter stopped on the path. "What did you say your name was?"

"Alice."

"Alice?" He spun on his heel and looked at her a moment as if trying to remember something, then quickly turned away. He took off his hat and ran his fingers through his hair again looking at the ground.

"Are you alright?" She asked.

"Yeah," he said turning again and smiling. "I was just trying to remember… where I saw your cat."

They walked several minutes past Merton College and down Rose Lane until reaching Magdalen College. Alice felt a twinge of excitement passing by the colleges where famous writers had lived and created entire worlds well known to her from childhood including Middle Earth and Narnia.

"This is *Mad-* len College," Carter said as he approached the closed gates.

"It is pronounced *Maud-len* College, I believe." Alice corrected.

The college was closed for the night but Carter opened his leather bag and brought out a large ring of keys. He quickly picked a key and unlocked the large wooden door. They walked through the stone building around the cloister lawn and out into the lush colorful garden.

"This way. I saw her along the Walk over the stream." He pulled out his ring of keys again and unlocked the large iron gate. They walked over the bridge and into the woods.

"I've never been this way before," Alice said, "What is this place?"

"It's Addison's Walk." Carter replied. "A long walk through the woods; the trail is one big circle. You end up right back here no matter which direction you go. Most people turn left, but I saw the cat down the trail this way." He turned right.

They walked for several minutes down the dirt path. Alice marveled at the beauty of the trees, the ivy, and the moss covered stones.

"So," Carter began as he slowed and walked beside Alice. "Where are you from?"

Alice scanned the bushes for her cat, wondering how she would ever find her in the thick ivy. "I'm from… well, London. I grew up there, mostly, we moved around a lot, but… what are you doing?" Alice noticed that Carter was chewing on something. "Is that? Is that a tea bag?" She made a face clearly showing her disgust.

"Yeah, what? You don't like to chew on tea?" He walked faster again. She was not sure she made the right decision walking out into the woods at night with a perfect stranger. She called after him. "You said you saw a

cat, but how can you know it was mine? Plenty of stray cats around, maybe you saw one of them."

"Not possible, it was your cat." Carter said walking back to her. "Let me see that picture again."

He reached out for the flyer in Alice's hand and before they even touched, a shock of electricity sent them both back a step.

"Whoa! That was some shock!" She said.

"It surprised me too," Carter said quietly. His dark eyes flashed and they appeared to have a light behind them. It seemed for a moment that his eyes betrayed something wild in him, something that made Alice uneasy.

"I was sure the cat would come once you were here. Maybe she'll only appear if you are alone. I promise I won't go far." Carter said suddenly and he turned off the path and walked into a clump of ivy disappearing behind the trees.

"Carter?" Alice called. She thought about turning and walking back. She was concerned about the coming darkness, and knew she should not be in the woods at night with a stranger. A strange stranger.

"*Alice!*" A soft whisper came from the trees. It sounded close yet distant. "*Alice, I'm here.*" The voice seemed so familiar. But it couldn't be… it couldn't be her sister. "*Alice, where are you?*" She spun around and could not see who was whispering.

"Oy, over here!" Alice turned again and saw Carter walking up from behind her. She sighed.

"Carter, what the Hell! You are freaking me out! I am leaving."

"I, uh…found your cat." Carter looked very grave at this point and Alice narrowed her eyes.

"Where?"

"I must insist you come with me to see her right away." He stared right into her eyes and she saw the same small light as before. She was mesmerized by it and at the same time disturbed.

"Is she alright?" Alice asked, a worry growing in her mind.

Carter turned to her with a serious look on his face. "Alice, I'm sorry but… I found her in the woods and she wasn't moving. Dyna is dead and I thought you should be the one to bury her. Come, she is right around the corner."

Chapter Two: An Upside Down Sea

Alice gasped and put her hand to her mouth. Carter led her over the bridge just to the left of the path. At the base of a tree in a bed of ivy lay a tabby cat, perfectly still, curled into a ball as if sleeping.

"Dyna!" Alice knelt beside her cat and wondered how she could have died. Did she suffer? Did she die of the cold, eat a toxic plant, or had some awful snake bitten her? Her eyes began to sting and she sniffed as the tears began to flow. She raised her hand to wipe her eyes but Carter took her hand and held it. As he took her hand she again felt a shock of electricity from his touch. He obviously felt it too and slightly jolted.

"It's ok," he said. "It's alright to cry at funerals."

Alice then wept. She cried for the loss of her cat, a constant companion for ten years, but she also cried for her sister, who had loved Dyna and played with her when she was only a kitten. She cried fearing that she would soon be attending another funeral, and would be left alone in the world. And she cried for herself, for losing her scholarship after her gymnastics injury, for the bitter breakup from her boyfriend after graduation, and for not knowing where her life was going or how she would pay all the bills that were mounting upon her. She cried for the sake of crying, letting all her emotions flow to the surface that had been seething beneath seemingly calm waters.

Finally, she looked up and noticed that Carter still held her hand. In his other hand he held a tea cup under her chin. He was staring at her with a sorrowful and inquisitive look on his face. The light in his eyes had dimmed. She looked down at the tea cup, which did not hold tea, but her tears. The cup was nearly half full and she wondered that she had cried so much.

"What are you doing?" Alice asked, immediately embarrassed that she had cried so openly in front of him and confused by the random appearance of the tea cup.

"Collecting your tears, of course. It is the only way back."

"I don't understand." She stood up quickly.

"I'm sorry about your cat, but I needed your tears, you see. Only your tears will open the way." Carter opened his leather satchel and pulled out a small vial of clear liquid. He poured it into the tea cup. Alice stepped backwards. Did he just imply that he killed her cat to make her cry? Carter placed his hat on his head and grinned.

"Thank you, Alice. I regret that we may never see each other again. Meeting you, I believe, was not chance. Please forgive me for deceiving you. I don't like the look of your face so sad. I hope that you will not cry so hard again, though for my sake, it was more than I hoped for."

He tipped his hat and brought the tea cup to his mouth. She realized this nut was about to drink her tears! The drink touched his lips, and Alice jumped back in terror as his body lifted from the ground and he was pulled inside the tea cup, his entire body up-ending so that his shoes disappeared last.

The cup hung in the air for only a moment, then fell straight to the ground, and landed flat, retaining the tears inside it. Alice stood staring at the place Carter had just been standing. Was she dreaming? She then knelt on her knees toward Dyna and in the dark reached out for her. Her body was still warm! Outrage came over her as she realized he must have killed Dyna just before coming to get her!

Alice's rage turned upon the tea cup. She seized it so forcefully, the thin porcelain shattered, spraying the tears into the air. Some of the water splashed into her face and she tasted the tears in her mouth. Suddenly she could see no more.

Her eyes went dark and her head began to spin. Alice felt coldness wrap around her and she could only hear a rushing sound in her ears. She could not tell if she was right side up or upside down, vertical, horizontal or diagonal. She was falling and spinning and then suddenly she was still, though her feet were not touching the ground. Alice opened her eyes and found herself up to her neck in deep water. She lifted her chin and breathed remembering to tread. She did not like swimming. Her greatest fear was drowning and she never swam in the deep end of a pool. At the seashore she would only put her toes in the water and she wore a life jacket whenever she went out on a boat, which was rare.

She began moving her arms and legs awkwardly in the water looking around her. There was no land in sight, no boats, no people. Just water and sky. In her thoughts she questioned how this reality could not be a dream. 'I have been drugged! Drugged and tossed out to sea. But how? Oxford is nowhere near the sea. How did I get here?'

Those thoughts were interrupted as Alice swallowed a mouth full of salt water and choked on it. Coughing, she began to panic. Her shoes fell off as she kicked and she pulled off the sweater that weighed her down. She tried to lie on her back and float. After several minutes, she felt very tired. Her arms and legs ached with strain, her shoulder erupted in spasms, and her head ducked under water a few times causing her pure terror.

"Help!" She cried out to nobody. "Somebody help me!"

Suddenly, a dolphin flew down through the air above her. It turned facing down, it's tail pointed up to the sky.

"You're a bizarre bird. Why are you flying upside down?" It asked in a squeaky voice.

Blinking the saltwater from her eyes, Alice was now sure this was a dream. "But I'm not upside down. You're the one upside down," she said dipping again beneath the water.

"No, I'm swimming. You're just hanging there. What are you doing up there?"

"I…" Alice's mind was consumed with trying to stay afloat and she could only answer. "I don't know!"

"Well, that is no good. You simply can't go on without a porpoise. I'm surprised you don't fall!"

She fell upwards into the sky as the world seemed to spin around one hundred and eighty degrees. Falling below (or above) the dolphin, Alice realized she could not breathe in the air and had an urgent desire to get back in the water that was above her. She tried to swim through the clouds back up to the water surface. The dolphin flew around her laughing and pushed her upwards. As Alice reached the water she pushed her head through the surface and found she could breathe easily. She tried to pull herself upward into the sea as she kept falling down back into the air. She found a piece of sea weed dangling like a vine and pulled herself up into the water. As she climbed the sea weed, schools of fish swam by upside down looking at *her* curiously.

'This dream makes no sense.' Alice thought. 'But when in a dream I rarely think that I am in one. How strange that I should wonder about the dream while still in it.' She continued to climb until, bumping her head on the ocean floor, a sea horse hanging upside down on

a bit of flotsam asked, "Are you a friend or anemone?" Alice stared at it and a sea star above her asked, "Have you ever wished upon a sea star?"

Alice shook her head then looked down and the world spun back around again. She found herself at the bottom of the sea unable to breathe! She swam up, this time without the help of anyone, determined not to drown. She could see the surface and only thought of the next stroke.

'Just one more,' she thought over and over. Her heart pounding and hands numb, she felt her lungs heave, commanding her throat to lurch and take in a breath, but she resisted. Upon reaching the surface, she gasped for air, taking in as much as her lungs would allow. It seemed that she would never catch her breath, but then she caught sight of something that made her swim as hard as she could. The shore. Alice found that she was surrounded on all sides by thick woods with a narrow beach circling what was now a small lake. Alice pulled herself into the sandy shallows and without resting, stood and walked from the waters' edge onto the grassy shore.

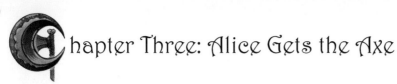

Chapter Three: Alice Gets the Axe

Alice had no shoes, no jacket, and no purse; three things she would never have left home without. She stood at the edge of the woods in the sun and brushed off as much sand from her dress and feet as she could. Turning towards the warm sun, Alice saw something moving on the opposite shore. It was a white rabbit, running on all fours through the low grass along the waters' edge. Its light color among the dark trees made it perfectly unmistakable. Alice watched as it ran along the lake and realized that it would soon reach her. She was suddenly startled by a loud blast from within the dark wood that rattled the trees and the white rabbit jumped in the air but kept running.

On the far shore, two red objects appeared. They were tall, had round red helmets and seemed to move smoothly over the terrain, as if floating. Then, three square white objects appeared in front of them. The two rounded red objects and the three white squares began fighting each other, until another loud blast shook the trees again and they all ran back into the woods. The white rabbit was getting nearer and Alice wasn't sure what to do. Should she get out of its way, try to help it, or should she be running too? As the rabbit approached, the blasts came nearer and each one caused it to jump in fear. Alice looked at it closer now and blinked. She blinked twice because the rabbit wore a waist coat. Another blast caused the rabbit to jump and this time it spoke.

"Got to get out!" It cried.

"Over here!" Alice called, though she didn't know what she could actually do to help. The White Rabbit stopped for a moment surprised, saying, "Alice! Where have you been? Where is the Watch?"

"Watch?" Alice asked, "What watch?"

"*The* Watch!" Another blast came from the trees and the White Rabbit squeaked nervously jumping in the air. He continued running and cried, "Hurry up! Must get out, now! Out of

Underland!"

Alice ran after him.

'Underland?' She thought. 'And the rabbit knows my name? Curious!' Through the trees a blast sounded very close, and she felt the ground and trees around her shake. The White Rabbit jumped and squeaked again and Alice continued to follow as fast as she could.

"Wait, please! Rabbit!" Alice called. She tried to keep up, but her bare feet were being cut by the thick ferns and branches on the forest floor. Alice thought it was strange because she had never felt pain in a dream before.

"Please wait!" She called out searching the green woods. Another blast caused the rabbit to jump in fright and Alice caught sight of the white flash of fur ahead of her. She ran only a few more strides to find a small clearing bordered with three large trees forming a triangle.

She spun in a circle to see where the White Rabbit had gone. To her left, Alice noticed a small door at the base of one of the trees. She crouched down on her knees and opened the little door that barely fit her head.

"Do you have my pocket watch?" The Rabbit cried running up to her. Alice turned her head at an awkward angle to see him.

"No, I haven't got it." Alice said.

"Well what did you do with it?" The White Rabbit cried.

"I don't know what you're talking about! I haven't ever had a pocket watch."

The Rabbit narrowed his eyes clearly implying she was lying. A blast came from behind the trees setting one tree on fire.

"Close the door!" He tried to push the door shut on Alice's head.

"Wait!" She held the door open. "How do I get out of… Underland?"

"Up the Rabbit Hole to the Surface! But you can't fit! Close the door!"

She wedged her elbow into the opening as the rabbit pushed and asked, "Where is the Rabbit Hole?"

"Down the Hall! Close the door, they are coming!" Giving up, the White Rabbit turned tail and ran down the long hallway disappearing around the corner. Two more loud blasts sounded close behind Alice. She quickly stood and, puzzled, she walked around the tree wondering how the hallway went back so far in such a small trunk.

Unexpectedly, she was seized by both arms as a booming voice came through the trees. "OFF WITH HIS HEAD!"

Alice looked back and saw that two oversized playing cards, each with arms, legs, and head, held onto her with great force. She twisted, attempting to wrench her arms from their grasp. Two other cards were crouched on the ground looking into the small open door.

Alice marveled at the giant cards. A Spade card had gotten its head stuck in the doorway and the cards holding her began to laugh. Struggling, she released one arm, smacked the card in the face and pulled her other arm free. Alice started to run but a massive red object blocked her way.

It was identical to a chess pawn, only this red creature had a face. The Pawn narrowed his eyes at her. She tried to push past it, but the Pawn was much stronger than the paper cards and he did not budge.

"Hey! She's *our* prisoner!" The number Two of Hearts called. The Spade card had freed itself and all four cards walked over.

The Pawn said, "Not anymore. She's going to the Red Queen." The Pawn pushed Alice forward with his bulky round body but the cards zipped in front of him and formed a wall with their bodies. "She's coming with us. The Queen of Hearts demands it."

"I do not take orders from a Queen of Hearts." The Pawn shoved Alice the other way but the cards whipped back around and formed the wall again. "We can do this all day you know, and when the Queen arrives, you might want to cover your neck."

"When the Red Queen arrives she'll blast you little cards to pieces."

"Well, when the Queen of Hearts arrives…"

"OFF WITH HIS HEAD!" The Queen of Hearts had arrived and she swung an enormous axe in her large left hand. The Pawn threw Alice to the ground just in time to have its head cleaved and it rolled across the forest floor and out of sight into the woods.

After a few seconds an explosion came from where the head rolled and the Queen mumbled, "I forgot about the exploding Pawn heads."

Alice stayed on her hands and knees, but looked up at the Queen of Hearts whose face turned red with anger at the sight of her.

"You!" The Queen of Hearts bellowed pointing a bony finger down at Alice. "You are the cause of all of this! You turned him against me!" Alice was surprised at being so accused. Looking down at her, the Queen grinned and Alice felt chills down her spine. "This time I have you! Where is the White Rabbit?"

Alice didn't say anything and looked back at the ground.

"WHERE IS THE WHITE RABBIT?!"

Shaking, she unthinking glanced at the little door.

The Queen chuckled, "Thank you, my dear. NOW GET IN THERE AND FIND HIM!" She ordered the cards. Several cards attempted to shove themselves in the door but they were all too big. One card folded itself twice over and another card pushed him in as far as he would go, but then it became stuck and could not unfold itself.

"IDIOTS!" The Queen walked over to the tree and began chopping it with her steaming hot axe. Alice watched helplessly as the axe crashed through the tiny door. The folded card was pulled out of the way just in time as the axe swung into the tree again and the hollow tree was completely taken down.

"DIG A HOLE! FIND THAT RABBIT!" The cards began digging around the tree. The Queen turned on Alice, "Once I have the Rabbit and the Watch, I WILL get my year back, and I shall take it from you! That will teach you not to touch things that aren't yours!"

"But I haven't done anything!" Alice cried in confusion

A card announced, "I found a hallway!"

Without warning, a loud blast sounded and the

trees near the Queen exploded in sparks and caught fire. The cards scrambled and fell over each other until they stood in front of the Queen creating a wall. Alice remained crouched on the ground behind them. Out of the woods came several red chess pieces including two Bishops with large spinning guns and two Knights hovering with sharp spinning blades rapidly rotating just above the ground. Through the guarding cards, she watched as the veiled Red Queen approached and recoiled at the sight of her.

The Red Queen spoke calmly and deliberately, "So, at last we have found the Rabbit Hole."

"HE IS NOT YOUR RABBIT, HE IS MY RABBIT!" The Queen of Hearts shouted.

"Shouting is not necessary." The Red Queen stood still as a statue. "I don't care about your insignificant rabbit. Now, what are you hiding back there?" The Red Queen turned her head slightly trying to see behind the cards.

"My prisoner," the Queen of Hearts said softly. Then she cried, "CLOSE THE WALL!" The cards straightened continuing to hide Alice from the Red Queen.

"I do not like your tone of voice. Not very queenly." The Red Queen's eyes were veiled, but she seemed to be staring at the spot Alice crouched.

The Queen of Hearts said, "She was a fugitive, and is now under arrest for theft, treason, sedition, rabbit-rousing, and for destroying my mirror!"

Alice huffed at these false accusations. The Red Queen's expressionless, veiled face stared at the Queen. "She destroyed your half of the Looking Glass?"

The Queen of Hearts raised her chin and her hand wrapped around a glass shard that hung from a black chain around her neck.

The Red Queen continued, "I would like to question your prisoner." At her word the two Bishops came forward aiming guns at the cards. The cards rippled but held the wall in front of Alice. A Castle moved quickly straight towards them, rotating its sickle blades and with cold calculation and a stone face, sliced one of the cards in half. The others looked at each other in terror but filled the gap and held fast.

The Castle raised its sickles again but the Queen of Hearts blocked it with the long handle of the axe and brought the steam-heated blade down upon the Castle's back. A dozen cards rushed in from the forest surrounding the chess pieces. The Red Queen raised a small brass gun and the cards all shuttered like a paper in a soft wind.

"I will not be troubled here." She said calmly. "I will be back to destroy the Rabbit Hole and anyone who stands in my way.

"YOU WILL DO AS I TELL YOU IN MY KINGDOM!" The Queen of Hearts lifted her axe and the dozen cards rushed upon the remaining chess pieces. Alice watched the battle surprised at the violence between paper and stone as the Knights and Bishops easily sliced through the cards, but then became overrun by sheer numbers. The Red Queen fired her strange gun sending half-a-dozen cards flying into the air on fire and she retreated into the woods. Alice was certain the Red Queen had not seen her. She slowly turned and tried to crawl away.

The Queen of Hearts spun around towards her and asked softly in a sickly sweet voice, "Where is the Watch?"

Alice turned back, confused. "I don't know." Alice answered. "I haven't got any watch."

The Queen raised her voice slightly. "You are a thief and a liar, now give me the Watch."

"I have no idea what you are talking about! What watch?" Alice felt frozen to the ground and her eyes shifted to the large steaming axe.

Turning red in the face, the Queen of Hearts pronounced in a screeching voice that nearly blasted Alice's hair back, "OFF WITH HER HEAD!" The Queen wielded the axe and lifted it high. Alice took in a breath, her eyes widening in fear when she was suddenly pulled out of the way, lifted up, and carried into the woods over a shoulder like a sack of potatoes. Her rescuer put her down and placed his finger to his lips. His dark eyes had a light deep within. "Carter!" Alice cried.

"Shh! Geez!" He placed a small clear vial in Alice's hand. "Drink it quick!"

He drank from his own small vial and instantly disappeared. She looked down and saw that the tiny glass in her hand said 'Drink Me'. The Queen bellowed wielding the axe towards her. Alice brought the vial to her lips and…

She felt herself falling.
down
down
down
down

down
down
down
down

She finally landed having never left the ground. She looked around in amazement. Everything was enormous; the pebbles were giant boulders, the sticks were logs, and the ferns were as high as the forest trees had been. She had shrunk to the size of a mouse.

"Over here, hurry!" Carter motioned to her from a hole underneath a rock. She ran to him and jumped into the hole. He lowered the rock over them and only a little light came through. Alice felt the ground shake and her ears were ringing with the booming sound of heavy footfalls upon the earth.

"WHERE ARE YOU?" The Queen of Hearts bellowed.

A Spade called out from the clearing, "My Queen! My Queen! We have the White Rabbit. We've dug him out, Your Highness."

The Queen of Hearts spun the axe through her fingers easily. "Excellent, take him to the castle! AS FOR YOU…" The Queen called out so loud Alice had to cover her ears. "I WILL FIND YOU AND YOU WILL PAY!" The Queen tromped away and Alice could hear the little squeaks of the White Rabbit being taken away.

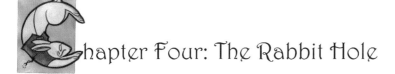

Chapter Four: The Rabbit Hole

Alice turned to Carter who was sitting comfortably on the ground sipping a cup of tea.

"You!" Alice sputtered. "You…you…"

"Saved your life, you're welcome."

"No, you…who are you?"

"I already told you." He put the empty tea cup in his pocket.

Alice looked at him incredulously. "Who are you, really?"

He stood up, his top hat knocking into the rock. He removed his hat checking it for damage. Then, pushing the rock up, he crawled out into the wood. He held out his hand for Alice but she climbed out of the hole on her own.

"Well?" Alice asked.

"Well, what?"

"Who are you really?" She demanded.

"Around here, they call me…Hatter."

Alice huffed, "As in the Mad Hatter?"

Hatter threw his hands in the air saying, "Why does everyone insist on calling me that? I mean I am a little mad I suppose, but who isn't? I don't go around adding adjectives to other people's names, like Irritating Alice!"

"What?" She'd had enough and crossed her arms glaring at him.

"Look, I'm sorry. This must all be very overwhelming for you. Let me explain." Hatter sat down on a dry leaf resembling a chair. He reached into his jacket pocket and pulled out another tea cup. Then he lifted his hat and pulled out a small bag of tea. He held his sleeve over the tea cup and hot water poured from his sleeve. He dropped in the tea bag and swirled the cup to stir it.

He finally said, "Nope, it's too much, I can't explain it." Hatter sipped his tea.

Alice placed her hands on her hips watching him, becoming more agitated and said, "You can explain why I am here in this crazy dream and why you are here in my dream. The last person I want to be dreaming about is you!"

"Dream?" Hatter looked amused.

Alice noticed a giant ladybug nearby crocheting a doily.

"Yes, dream! And any moment I'll wake up and be back with Lorina and Dyna… Hey! You killed my cat!" Alice again felt the anguish of losing her cat and thoughts of her fading sister flashed into her mind.

"You murderer! What did you do to her?" She yelled so loudly a giant grasshopper suddenly leapt from where he had been resting and landed on a twig that snapped, and half of it flung through the air nearly taking Hatter's hat off.

"I did not kill your cat!" Hatter exclaimed. "Dyna is fine; I only gave her some lavender tea to make her sleep."

"She's only sleeping?" Alice's heart rose to sudden joy. She longed to have Dyna back safe in her arms, if she could only wake up." Is that what you gave me?" She asked with narrowed eyes. "Something in the tea? And now I'm here drugged, sleeping in the middle of the woods late at night…"

Hatter adjusted his hat. "Look, you're not sleeping; you followed me in. You're back now!"

Alice was very confused by this and began pinching herself to wake up. Hatter stood and put his full cup of tea in his pocket. "Hey, everything is alright. I had no idea you could come through the Pool of Tears too!"

"The what?" She asked.

"The Pool of Tears; a portal between worlds. Well, from the Surfaceland to the Underland. Only it takes two sets of tears to work. When I found *you*, I knew you were my ticket home. But I needed to make you cry. I'm sorry about tricking you, Alice."

"So you put your tears in the cup too?" She asked.

"For the portal to open both tears must be from someone who has been in here before. Don't you see? We are back in wonderful Underland!" Hatter spun around with his arms outstretched. "And now I have a chance to be free again. Thanks to you!"

"Wonderful Underland? As in Wonderland?" Alice asked in disbelief.

"Don't you remember?" He asked. "Haven't you been here before?"

"Of course I haven't been here before! And who were all those crazy people and what did they want with me?"

"You must have just been in the wrong place at the wrong time. It appears the Queens are after the White Rabbit. He's been going back and forth through a portal for years, and the Red Queen now wants all the Portals destroyed. The Queen of Hearts was after the White Rabbit too, though I have no idea why. I thought the Rabbit worked for her." Hatter looked up in thought.

"Change me back!" Alice demanded.

"Why? We're safer like this. Our walk will be a little longer, but…"

"We need to go after them!" She pointed the direction the Queen had stomped off.

"Go after them! After you just escaped having your head chopped off? That is one paper cut I do not want."

"They captured the White Rabbit!" She cried.

"*I* don't care." Hatter replied.

"Do you care about anything?"

"Cup of tea?"

"Ooo, you are infuriating!" Alice stomped her foot.

"Me? You are the one who got the Queen in a tizzy, you led them to the Rabbit Hole, and now you want to go back? No thank you, Irritating Alice. You can go on your own."

"Fine! Mad Hatter! I will!" She crossed her arms and turned to go.

Hatter sighed, ran in front her and said in a much calmer tone, "Wait. Ok, I'm sorry. Didn't mean to call you that, although I do like the look on your face when you are angry." Hatter grinned.

Alice fumed.

Hatter said, "Look, you cannot simply run after the Queen of Hearts and rescue a prisoner. Underland is mad, but it has rules, and the rules are: you don't mess with the Queen of Hearts. Her House of Cards is the most powerful House in Underland and though the Queen is cracked, she is very dangerous."

"But it's my fault! The White Rabbit had lost his watch and if I hadn't followed him the Queen might not have caught him! Plus, how will I get up the Rabbit Hole without him? I must get back home, you see. I haven't much time…" Alice thought about her sister in the hospital.

"The White Rabbit lost his Watch? That is very interesting." Hatter thought a moment, "Hmm, I wonder if it might still be there somewhere! Come on!" Hatter stood and walked back towards the clearing.

"Where are you going?" Alice asked.

"The Rabbit Hole, of course. We've got to get you home. I've never seen inside a rabbit's hole and I am rarely this size. Follow me."

Hatter started walking towards the clearing. Alice struggled over the large branches and spongy detritus in her bare feet and strapless dress. Hatter offered his hand over every puddle and pebble, but Alice stubbornly refused his help.

Looking up at the towering treetops, Alice thought how frightening she must look to every small creature whenever she walked through the woods. She was amazed by the detail of the ferns and how large drops of water hung upon the leaves without spilling. She wondered how much she weighed and imagined that a strong gust of wind might sweep her up and drop her where ever it pleased.

As they reached the clearing, Hatter hid behind a small stone and motioned for Alice to stay still.

"The Queen of Hearts left two Suits behind," he whispered. "We'll have to get past the guards to get in."

Alice saw two of the oversized playing cards staring ahead on either side of the chopped up tree trunk. The little door was smashed to pieces. Hatter picked up a large leaf from the ground and lifted it over his head.

"What are you doing?" Alice asked.

"We are going to be little insects and make our way to the broken door. If we walk up behind them, they'll never notice us. So not a word until we get inside." He flashed a smile and swiftly turned. She apprehensively followed him around the edge of the woods until they reached the back of the tree. Hatter lifted the leaf up and was about to head for the broken door but Alice stopped him.

"Wait. Carter…Hatter, why are you doing this? Why are you helping me?"

"Why?" Hatter looked insulted. "Why would I not help you? I am the reason you are here and I shall assist you in your swift return home. Dyna, I am sure, has already awoken and waits for you at your doorstep."

Alice did not believe for a moment that he would risk his own life for her. She raised her eyebrows and he tried again. Leaning in close, he said, "Look, I know how it is to be trapped in a world that is not your own. You clearly feel you don't belong here, and I'll get you out if I can, 'kay?"

Alice had no choice but to go along with him and hope she could get up the Rabbit Hole. She also pinched herself hoping she would wake up. Hatter lifted the leaf over his head

and she ducked beneath it. Together they moved slowly to the broken door. Alice did not take her eyes off the giant guards who could easily stomp her out of existence with a misplaced foot. Reaching the broken door, they quickly stepped inside.

Alice was careful not to hook her dress on the shattered pieces of wood that littered the entry way. Keeping the leaf over their heads, Hatter continued on past the open ceiling of the chopped trunk and into the hallway. Alice assumed they must be underground now and the hallway seemed to grow larger as they walked, as if the walls were stretching out like a large balloon.

Then it suddenly came to an end and as he turned the corner, Hatter shouted,

"Ha!" Down a short length of hallway that continued to stretch upwards, they came into a very large room with a table and pictures and a ceiling so high Alice could not see the top.

"It must be here somewhere!" Hatter exclaimed as he walked around the room.

"What?" Alice asked staring up into the ceiling.

"The, er, way up Rabbit Hole, of course." Hatter replied.

"What are you really looking for, Hatter?" Alice did not trust him at all.

He sighed, "You said the Rabbit lost his Watch, but did he say where he thought it was?"

"The watch?" She asked confused. "Why do you care about the watch?" She was not about to tell him that the White Rabbit thought *she* had the watch.

Hatter turned away quickly. "This is just silly. We can't find anything like this." He took a small piece of cake from his pocket and bit into it, instantly growing to his full height! Hatter adjusted his hat and looked around the room again, this time checking behind the paintings and opening the drawers of a chest that Alice only then noticed. His significantly larger yellow shoes tromped all around and Alice had to run under the table to keep from being squashed. She called up to him as loud as she could several times but could not make him hear her.

Finally, he bent down and lowered his hat for Alice to climb on. Bringing her eye level, Hatter whispered so as not to harm her ears, "The Rabbit Hole goes so far up I cannot see how the rabbit climbed up it. There seems to be no path."

Hatter lifted her as high as he could. Alice looked up the dark hole in the ceiling that did not end. Straining her eyes she could see no light at the end and nothing to hold onto, no climbing rope, no ladder.

"How could the rabbit have climbed this?" She asked aloud. Hatter heard her this time, being so close to his ear.

"He may have gone another way, or maybe he hopped?"

Alice heard a buzzing sound coming from the wall. "Do you hear that? What could that noise be?"

Hatter put his hat on his head and turned towards the sound. It slowly grew louder and louder, then large spinning blades sliced down into the room followed by dozens of flying shards of glass that cut through one of the portraits and shattered the small table.

"Knights!" Hatter said. "They're here to destroy the Rabbit Hole!" The blades swung through again, this time barely missing Hatter's hat which Alice perched upon. "We need to get out of here!" Hatter was now too big to go back through the hallway, and shards of glass sticking out of the walls and floor made it impassable. He ran to the back wall beneath the Rabbit Hole and dodged the flying glass when a blast from above sent him sliding across the floor. Alice held on to a hat pin and watched as blast after blast knocked openings into the Rabbit Hole. Furniture fell from the darkness including tables, chairs, bookshelves and framed paintings. Couches, lamps, armoires and potted plants all fell creating a huge pile of broken debris. Finally, mounds of earth fell from the hole and then piles of grass and tree roots stacked up to the ceiling and beyond. The Rabbit Hole had been filled.

Another blast knocked an opening in the wall just next to where Hatter was standing. A Bishop holding a large gun came through the wall and Hatter punched him in the face. The Bishop did not flinch and Hatter doubled over cradling his hand from having punched stone. Then he grabbed the Bishop's arm, slammed his fist into the metal elbow joint and twisted the arm so the gun pointed back. He pulled the pin that locked the gun to the Bishop's arm and pressed the trigger. The Bishop blew backwards out through the wall and Hatter pocketed the bronze gun.

Wasting no time, he took a bright blue bit of chalk from his coat. He ran up to the back wall and drew a long rectangle. Alice held on to the hat pin to keep from rolling off. Hatter hastily colored in the rectangle and then drew a circle on the left hand side.

"Is that a door?" Alice asked without being heard. Several Knights sliced through the walls into the Rabbit Hole and a Pawn head rolled through the blown-out wall then stopped.

Hatter pounded on the wall as hard as he could. Nothing happened. Alice realized the Pawn's head had a sparkling fuse.

"Hurry!" She shouted as she watched the fuse burn down. Frustrated, Hatter kicked the blue door knob and his foot went straight through the wall as the door opened.

He pulled his leg out of the wall and ran through the door into a shop full of very angry creatures. Alice watched in amazement as Hatter kicked the door closed behind him just as the Pawn-head bomb exploded.

Chapter Five: The Hatter House

Taking a breath, Alice found herself in a shop full of oddly shaped hats with many creatures already in the process of queuing to complain. She looked back and saw that there was no longer a door, no Rabbit Hole, just a black scorch mark on the wall. Hatter told everyone to get out, that the shop was closed and no one was going to get what they wanted. A giant pelican angrily snapped his bill at Hatter saying, "My order is so late, I can't recall what I ordered; but I want it now!" This set off another yelling match of the creatures in the shop that included an osprey, an aardvark, a turtle, a porcupine, and a kinkajou; all creatures Alice remembered seeing at the zoo in London as a child.

"I've only just got back and the store is still closed! Now everybody clear off!" Hatter pushed past them and walked briskly out of the shop and through the small village.

"Will you stop and put me right?" Alice yelled, starting to feel queasy riding around on the hat. "Where are we? How did we get here? How am I going to get home now?" She cried. Hatter put up his hand and she stepped onto it.

"Which do you want me to answer first?" He asked while bringing her down to his eye level.

She tried to remember what she had already asked and ventured, "Change me back, first."

Hatter bent and placed her on the ground. He took out a crumb from his pocket and holding it between his thumb and forefinger, he let Alice take it from him.

"Just a little, it's all I have left," he said.

To Alice the crumb was nearly a hand full. She took one big bite and felt herself shoot up like she had been shot from a canon! She suddenly stood nose to nose with Hatter and he quickly took a step back in surprise. Recovering, he said, "Whoa, that was a little too close! I should think to step a little farther back next time." He took a cup of tea from his hat and sipped it.

"There will not be a next time!" Alice exclaimed. "Now tell me what happened and where we are?"

"I used Knock Chalk, it opens a door, but that door will only lead to the last place it was used. I guess I last used it to get out of that abhorrent Hat Shop."

"And how am I supposed to get home now if I can't get up the Rabbit Hole?" Alice was becoming very tired of this dream and pinched her arm. "Oww!"

Hatter stopped Alice from pinched herself further, grabbing her hand then quickly letting go. Alice flinched at his touch expecting a shock, but no shock came.

He said, "We'll just have to find another way to get you home. I think I know someone who might help you. Or not. Depends on his mood. And we might not be able to find him. He usually has to find you, but I think he'll be curious about you." He grinned as he walked Alice down the path away from the crowd of creatures that had gathered to look at her.

"Curious? About me?" Asked Alice, noticing the congregating assembly.

"Believe it or not, it is rare that an outsider comes down into Underland." Hatter quickened his step and rounded the corner of the street leading Alice into a path lined with an orange picket fence.

"Who is this person we are meeting?" She asked.

"Not a person. You'll see. First we need to get some things. We're going to stop at my house on the way."

"Your house? You have a house?"

"Of course, silly. Where else would I live?" He opened a small gate at the end of the path and led Alice through a garden of colorful flowers. She looked twice at the flowers to

discover they were actually tea cups growing on long green stems. Some tea cups were smaller than a finger nail and others were larger than a cat. A brown butterfly landed on one of the tea cups and was soon joined by several others. Looking closer, Alice discovered each had a sugar cube head and wings like thin bread slices. Together they formed a small loaf of bread and one dipped its sugar cube head into the tea and flew off, followed by the others. "A BreadandButter Fly," Hatter commented seeing Alice's wonder. "They are very common in tea gardens."

They quickly walked past a house with long brown rabbit ears growing out of the roof. Next to the house was a large, long table, set for at least twenty people with a different colored wing-back armchair at each place.

"Is someone having a party?" Alice asked.

"No!" Hatter abruptly answered and then said no more about it. The mismatched dishes appeared to have not been used in some time as they were faded and coated in a layer of dust.

Down a short stone path and around several large trees, a tall house emerged and Alice stood for a moment in awe. Green ivy crawled up three stories of the otherwise dark yellow siding and the whole structure seemed to lean to one side. The faded yellow shingles were dislodged and looked as if a strong wind would send them sliding down the sloping roof of the crooked third story. She imagined that the sprawling ivy was the only adhesive keeping the house upright.

Hatter waited at the door, and then shut the door behind them as they walked through the entryway. The first floor was quite straight. The only hint at the upper stories imbalance was a thin crack in the ceiling that spider-webbed across the hallway. The spiraling stairs leading up tilted but had several books underneath one end to even it out.

"I know, I know," said Hatter watching Alice observe the room. "The whole house is in disrepair. I simply haven't been able to fix anything during Tea Time. I've been meaning to call 'round someone to do the cleaning but… exile kinda put a damper on my plans." Hatter continued to mutter as he opened a small closet door and walked inside. Alice peered in and saw that the closet was enormous and filled with colorful coats and large hats. Hatter emerged and held out a blue coat. "I think that will fit you." He quickly handed the coat to Alice and excusing himself, he sprinted up the crooked stairs.

She put the coat on and found it very soft and comfortable. She buttoned up the fitted coat and found that it suited her perfectly. In the main sitting room, there were several very plush couches, two armchairs, and everywhere were small tables with tea cups and settings for tea time. Alice wondered about the time and looked for a clock. She could not find one anywhere and finally came across a silver pocket watch on one of the small tables. It had been smashed and looked as if it were coated with old crusted strawberry jam.

Alice wondered about the White Rabbit's missing watch. Why had he thought she had it? Why did the Queen think she knew where it was? The Queen had called her a thief. Had the watch

been stolen? If it wasn't her, which Alice was sure it was not, who *did* steal it? And what was so important about a stupid little pocket watch?

Hatter came back down the crooked stairs. "Here try these on." Hatter tossed Alice a pair of boots. She tried them on, and though they were a little big, they felt comfortable.

"Ah! You have no idea how good it feels to be home again!" Hatter cried dramatically and fell into one the couches. He put his feet up and lay back looking at the ceiling. "I missed you, house!"

Suddenly a little mouse jumped up on the couch and squeaked loudly. Hatter stood excitedly. "Dormouse, my little bat! Whatever have you been at?" He grabbed the little mouse in his hands and looked wildly around the room. Finding what he was looking for, Hatter ran to a copper, bubbling teapot, lifted the lid and shoved the mouse inside. He slammed on the lid and laughed as he picked up the teapot and poured hot tea out of it into a porcelain cup.

Alice gasped thinking he had just drowned the mouse in boiling water, but the little mouse stuck its head out of the teacup and grinned. It jumped out perfectly dry onto the tea cup plate as Hatter lifted it and began sipping the tea.

"Care for a tea, Alice? Plenty of room, you know." He gestured at the many seats.

She sat down and he poured her a cup of tea. "Sugar?" Alice nodded. Hatter reached into a nearby flower vase and pulled out two sugar cubes. "Cream?" She nodded again mostly from a curiosity of where Hatter would get the cream from. Hatter reached past Alice, leaned over her quite close and picked up a small candle holder filled with cream and poured it into her cup. Hatter sat down very pleased with himself. "I have so missed my own tea."

Alice held her tea waiting for it to cool and asked, "Why are you always drinking tea?"

His smile faded as an unpleasant memory crossed his face and he said, "It is always time for tea."

"How can that be? Tea time is only once a day."

Hatter looked very seriously at her as if deciding whether or not to divulge a great secret. "I am cursed by Time, Alice. I fought with Time and lost. He has punished me forever with a party that never ends. Kind of like an addiction, I must have tea constantly."

"Isn't there anything you can do about it?" She asked confused.

"Yeah, I can find Time again and ask him to restart time for me. I'm frozen you see, frozen at Tea Time."

"So very strange to be frozen at a time of day! Doesn't your clock tell you when tea time is over?"

"Clocks!!" Hatter yelled at the top of lungs causing the dormouse to jump from the plate into Alice's tea.

Hatter spotted the jam encrusted pocket watch and grabbed it, smashed it into floor then placed it in a black tea pot of boiling water. Calmly, he sipped his tea before continuing. "Clocks are controlled by Time and do not move for me. They pass the hour, perhaps, but they never allow it to be any other time but Tea Time." Hatter stood up and paced agitated. "Do you have any idea how difficult it is to keep this up? Always Tea Time? Constantly drinking tea and eating nothing but bread with butter and jam and cakes and those awful little sandwiches without crust! It's enough to make one mad!"

The Dormouse floated on his back in Alice's tea enjoying the warmth and he dreamily sank into the dark water.

"What I wouldn't give for dinner time! Stews and roast turkeys and potatoes and wine. Oh! For a glass of wine! Or breakfast time! Sausages and eggs and bacon and waffles and omelets and juice!"

Hatter sat back down calm now, but in a cheerless mood. "It's easier here, at home. I can keep tea in my pocket and conjure cups and scones. On the Surfaceland it costs me a fortune having to buy everything and it's hard to keep a real job when I must eat and drink all day long! Sleep is my only peace, but I can't sleep for long and I wake up with terrible cravings! That's why I worked at Café Loco, for the tea! Although the décor wasn't bad either."

Hatter sighed, "Time is stopped for me, so I don't gain weight, my teeth don't rot out or turn brown, my hair doesn't change color, I don't age…"

"You don't age!" marveled Alice. "How old are you then?" She asked hoping she wasn't being too rude.

"I don't know. Could be fifty years, could be hundreds. Lost count, I guess. I don't remember ever having counted."

"But you were a child here, weren't you?"

"I don't know, I don't remember being a child. I hardly remember a time before time stopped for tea. Nothing ever changes, but nothing is ever the same."

Chapter Six: Time and Tea Cups

Alice placed her tea cup on the small table next to her as the Dormouse swam around happily. She listened as Hatter told her about all that had happened to him as far back as he could remember.

"I was falsely accused!" He continued to explain that Time was already upset with him from an incident with The Queen of Hearts when, orders piling up at the hat shop, he said aloud that he 'never had enough time!' Time himself arrived and Hatter accused Time of speeding up when he was behind in his work and slowing down whenever he boiled water for tea.

"We were friends once. I made him a very good hat, one of my best. But I was impatient and I accused him of being relative." Hatter shook his head remembering his greatest blunder.

"A relative of whom?" The Dormouse squeaked.

"Exactly!" Hatter pointed at him as if he understood completely. "Time argued that he did no such thing and that the clock remained as constant as love and as predictable as death. Then he asked me how much time I thought I needed and I replied, 'Just enough to take a break for tea.' From that moment it was always tea time and I have not been able to work since. My customers have been so angry. It was very difficult at first, keeping up with constant tea time."

"What did you do?" Alice asked astonished by his affliction.

"I once held a tea party that lasted a very long time. My friend the March Hare helped me devise a system of replacing cups easily by setting the table for twenty, when it was only the two of us!"

"Where is the March Hare now?" Alice had never heard such a tale before and truly felt for Hatter's situation, however absurd it seemed.

"The March Hare doesn't come around anymore," he said sadly.

"Why not?"

"He owes me a penny!"

"Only a penny? For what?"

"He asked me, 'A penny for your thoughts?' So I put my two cents in, then he left with the other penny!" Hatter stood up agitated and tensely walked up and down the sitting room.

"I'm sorry." Alice did not want to see him so stressed. "Can you not apologize to Time?"

"I have tried, but Time is hard to catch up with. It was in my last attempt that I was banished by the Queen of Hearts. If she found out I'd returned…" Hatter put down his tea cup and the dormouse bounded from Alice's cup into his pocket.

"Why were you banished by the Queen?" Alice asked, but Hatter was looking out the window. A small turtle was pointing at the house as several Suits walked up behind it.

Hatter said, "Now that you've finished your tea, we need to go."

"But I haven't had any tea."

He took Alice by the hand and pulled her out the back door. She dropped her cup and looked back as they ran towards the old Tea Table. Several cards had broken the front door of Hatter's house and rushed inside.

Hatter exclaimed, "I left my bag!" He pulled Alice underneath the Tea Table.

"I hope they don't go onto the third floor," he said watching his house anxiously.

Alice heard a massive crack. The third floor slid off the house and crashed in a cloud of ivy and yellow paint dust. Hatter sighed and got up from underneath the table. He looked sadly at the house and then turned to the old and broken cups and pots.

"Underland is getting old without me." Hatter turned and led Alice past the March Hare house and back through the garden.

"Hatter, I'm sorry about your house." Alice was sure the cards had been looking for her.

"They would have come for me eventually, Alice. Now we must hurry; we don't want to cross the Boards at night.

"Where are we going?" Alice asked.

"Why is a Raven like a writing desk?" Hatter asked. The dormouse popped his head out of Hatter's jacket pocket to listen.

"Hmm, a riddle?" Alice thought about it and could only come up with a couple of similarities. "Because they both are covered in black ink? Or because they both produce flat notes?" Alice thought she was rather clever for that one.

"No." Hatter said. The Dormouse ducked his head inside the pocket again. She continued to try and think of answers as they walked down a winding path that soon became stone steps over a stream, and then into a valley with strangely cut grass. As she observed the valley in the distance it appeared that the land was divided into large squares, like a chess board.

"Come on, we don't want to spend too much time on the Board. This land is the White Queen's land. And though she is not as murderous as the Red Queen, we still do not want to be stopped by her Pawns."

Alice hurried behind Hatter and they crossed the field quickly. "I've got it!" She said as they reached the shadow of several tall dark trees.

"Why is a raven like a writing desk? Because Edgar Allen Poe wrote about a raven *on* a writing desk!"

"No," Hatter grinned. "But that was a good one. Any other guesses before I tell you the answer?"

Alice sighed, "Because both have feather quills?"

"No. Because they are both made of wood." Hatter bowed giving the answer.

"But that makes no sense," she said. "Raven's are not made of wood."

"This one is. Welcome to Ravenwood." Hatter turned towards the trees and Alice realized they were at the threshold of a large forest.

"I remember coming to Ravenwood often before Tea Time, but I don't remember why or what for. I do remember, however, this is where we can find the Cheshire Cat. I was good at finding cats."

"Cheshire Cat? Is that his name?"

"I don't know his name. But he may know how to get you home… and other things."

They walked into the woods and Alice marveled at the many strange creatures along the path including hedgehogs with cotton candy on their backs instead of spines, birds that had opened feathers into folding chairs allowing small lizards to sun themselves, and squirrels that had paint brushes for tails which they dipped in the different colored paint flowers then scattered paint on all the trees. The colors would glisten like dew drops then fade away.

"Why is this place called Ravenwood?" Alice asked.

"Because if you spend too much time in this wood," Hatter answered, "it is said you start acting like a Raven Lunatic."

Alice smiled and shook her head.

After several hours of aimless walking, she sighed loudly and sat down on a rock rubbing her shoulder. "I'm very tired, Hatter. Can we take a rest? I can't walk another step!"

She took off the slightly too large left boot and rubbed her foot.

Hatter sat down and had a cup of tea. "I don't know why he hasn't come yet. I was sure he'd appear once you entered the wood. Maybe he will only appear if you are alone." He thought about it for a moment and decided. "I'm going to walk away for a little   while, not too far though, and if I find the Cat I'll bring him to you. If he arrives here, try to keep him talking until I return."

"How long will you be? I don't want to be left alone here, what if something happens?" Alice looked around at the small clearing and realized the sun was low in the sky. She certainly did not want to be alone in the dark in a strange wood.

Hatter said, "I promise I won't go far, I'll collect some wood for a fire tonight and be back before the sun sets. If you need anything just call me, I'll hear you."

"How will you hear me?" She asked realizing he meant to sleep out here over night.

"I'll be listening."

He disappeared into the trees and Alice shivered pulling her coat closer around her even though it was not cold. She then noticed a large mushroom the size of a tree trunk on the other side of the clearing and watched as a tiny green grasshopper landed on it. The Grasshopper began rubbing its back legs together making a loud chirping sound. Then another grasshopper landed on the mushroom top and began chirping. Soon the clearing seemed to be surrounded by grasshoppers and crickets and katydids all creating a cacophony of discordant sounds. Several frogs began a low throated call and other strange noises poured into the wood now. The flowers on the trees were swaying and even jumping with the notes. No, the flowers were making the music! Trumpet flowers played chromatic scales while Fluted Gum trees flouted high pitched squeaks. The Triangle Goldeneye chimed in, the Drumstick Primrose rolled a beat, and the Fiddle Leaf Fig struck a chord. Alice realized the jarring sound was equal to an orchestra tuning up. Finally, the small Blue Bells rang out a high note and all sound stopped.

The crickets and katydids turned toward a large pink Begonia that held a small reed like a baton in its leaf. Raising the baton, the Begonia motioned for the strings to begin. The Viola Grasshoppers and Violin Crickets came in with a slow beautiful harmony. The Cello Katydids came in after four measures as the frogs croaked out the bass and soon the percussion, winds, and horns joined in the woodland symphony. A tiny Fluted Flower piped in with a piccolo solo and a frog tenor burst out a harmony while a mantis played a piano concerto. As the sun continued to descend, Alice listened enthralled trying to hear each flower's tune and discover which bug was the first chair soloist. She swayed to the music and then stood as the sound became more sweeping and melodic inspiring her to dance on the soft grass. Damselflies waltzed through the air in fine gowns as she gracefully twirled, the setting sun's rays of pink and orange hues cutting through the thick foliage and illuminating the small clearing with a radiance that danced off Alice's pale complexion giving her a soft glow among the night flowers.

Hatter returned then, and silently watched Alice dance to the music of the wood. Alice playfully touched one of the dandelions, startling it, sending the feathery white seedlings into the air. She blew the seedlings away and discovering they had wings, the seedlings flew into the treetops. Alice laughed, for a moment forgetting her sister, forgetting her pain and her obligations, forgetting she was far from home and just danced, reveling in the cool breeze flowing through her hair and the touch of the soft grass on her feet. Finally, as the sun set, the flowers began to close their petals and the grass hoppers, crickets, and katydids leapt away to find shelter for the coming night.

Alice sat down upon the large mushroom and Hatter approached her, his arms full of thick branches. She smiled at him and he only nodded before dropping the firewood down. He quickly set to work starting the fire and remained silent, though he glanced back at several times as Alice watched. Once the fire had caught onto the wood, Hatter sat back on the grass and took off his hat. A tea cup rested on his head. Hatter quickly took it and from his pocket drew two lumps of sugar.

"How do you do that?" Alice asked.

"What?"

"How do always have tea cups everywhere? And where does the hot water come from?"

"Alice, how can I answer that question? Why it's silly! It just… is. That's all. There is no why or how or who or what or when. Only, *it is*."

Alice shook her head. "That's nonsense, everything has an explanation."

"Alright," Hatter turned to her and she came down from the mushroom to sit opposite him by the fire. "Tell me this, why did you cry so much into the tea cup?"

Alice frowned, "Because…thanks to you, I thought my cat was dead. And I loved her."

"Is that all? Because it seemed that you cried for more than her." He sipped his tea.

"I cried because… because she isn't the only one I've lost recently. But you wouldn't understand love."

"Love?" He looked up very interested now. The Dormouse popped his head out of Hatter's jacket pocket. "I think I know about love. It is said to be as fleeting and inconstant as Time or it the most powerful force in the Universe. But where does it come from? What is love?"

"Love is…" Alice suddenly felt the cold night chill and tucked her legs under her moving closer to the fire. Memories of her first boyfriend streamed through her, moments she now knew were false promises. Thoughts of her sister, and imagining life without her, tightened her throat and she could only speak loud enough for Hatter to just hear.

"Love is the feeling that there is more to you than yourself, like you were meant for something greater. That someone else is a part of you and that is the more essential part." She felt tears stinging at her eyes. "Love is feeling that your chest will explode if you can't share it and…it is like a house falling on you when it is lost." She wiped her eyes to keep tears from flowing.

Hatter put his tea down and got out another cup, offering it to Alice. She took the hot tea gratefully. He asked, "But why do we fall in love? Who controls that part?"

"I don't know what makes us fall in love. We just do." Alice blew on the hot tea and took a sip.

"We just do." Hatter answered, the firelight flickered in the reflection of his dark eyes. "Like your dancing. You love to dance, no reason for it. You just do. It just is."

Alice blushed and turned her head toward the fire.

"I'm sorry, I saw you dancing as I walked up, I didn't mean to…"

Alice felt silly about being embarrassed. She took several more sips from her tea cup.

"It was amazing that the forest should be able to make such beautiful music. I wished…" Alice yawned suddenly, "that it would go on forever." She felt very sleepy and her head felt so heavy she had to lie down in the grass.

"Alice?" Hatter asked.

Alice's eyes began to close and for a moment she wondered if Hatter had tricked her again. "What…" she asked as she drifted to sleep, "What did you put in my tea?"

Chapter Seven: The Cheshire Cat

Alice awoke in the morning light, the fire out and her jacket laid over her like a blanket. She sat up wondering what time it was but didn't dare ask Hatter.

"Finally!" He said. "I thought you'd never wake up."

She turned to find the large mushroom was laid out with an excellent arrangement of scones, strawberries, butter, jam, tea and cream. The Dormouse sat on the table munching a biscuit. Very hungry, Alice jumped up to the table but felt a twinge of pain in her shoulder. She rubbed her muscles grimacing.

"Are you alright?" Hatter asked.

"I have some issues with my shoulder. I injured it a year ago." Alice pushed the awful memories of the Gymnastics Nationals aside. Because of her injury, she could never compete again.

"Tea?" Hatter offered.

"No thank you," she answered curtly.

"What's wrong?" He asked.

"The tea." Alice said shortly." The tea made me fall asleep last night. What did you put in it?"

"I didn't put anything in the tea." Hatter said. "It was a calming tea. I guess it *was* rather strong."

Alice frowned remembering that her cat was probably still sleeping in the woods or worse, awake and lost again.

"Alice." Hatter began, sensing her suspicion. "Do you think I would hurt you? Do you not trust me?"

She asked, "Why were you looking for the White Rabbit's watch back at the Rabbit Hole? What is so important about it?"

He sighed, "It was just a fool's hope. That Watch is *the* time keeper of Underland. Time himself keeps that watch. If I had it, and broke it, Time would come to fix it and then I could force him to take away my curse. But Alice," Hatter leaned over the mushroom table. "I would never do anything to harm you. I'm trying to help you, aren't I?"

Alice was silent and ate her scones dry. She wondered what Hatter would think if he knew the Queen of Hearts thought she stole the Watch. Though he offered again, she refused the tea. He was just explaining the plan for the day, which included a lot of walking around aimlessly, when Alice heard a faint humming in the trees.

"Hatter, what is that?"

"What is what?"

"That humming. Don't you hear it?" The humming became louder but Hatter shook his head. Alice spun around as the sound seemed to be coming from all directions.

"It's him." Hatter said, looking wary. "It must be him."

A voice sang echoing through the woods.

"Tweedle Dee, Tweedle Dum. The Walrus calls all to come. Oysters follow when they should run. The Carpenter too eats every one."

"Did you hear that?" Cried Alice.

Hatter shook his head. "No, he may only appear to you. Tell me if you see him!"

"Where are you?" Alice asked.

"Here, there, and everywhere."

She spun around trying to pin-point the voice.

"There was a cat caught in tree, nothing would get him to move, the fool climbed up to get him out and now she's stuck there too!"

Alice looked up in the tree and saw a brightly colored striped cat dangling from the branches smiling down at her with a wide toothy grin.

"There he is!" She called to Hatter and pointed up in the tree. But the cat was gone.

"Over here, deary dear." The cat suddenly appeared in another tree swooshing his bushy tail back and forth.

"Don't go! I need to ask you a question!" Alice ran over to the tree.

"Questions are infinite, answers only raise more questions."

"Please! I want to find a way out of this crazy Wonderland."

"Why?"

"To get home?"

"Why?"

"Because people will be worried about me."

"Who?"

"My fam…" Alice stopped unable to answer. Lorina was her only family and since the accident, Alice had pulled away from friends. But she was sure someone would notice when she didn't show up for work.

The Cheshire Cat swished his tail and turned his head nearly upside down looking at her. She turned her head sideways to look at him and asked, "What is your name, Cheshire Cat?"

"Hmm," the Cheshire Cat purred. "I will tell you if you can answer me one question positively."

Alice raised her eyebrows at the challenge and nodded.

"Can you stand on your head?" The Cheshire Cat asked and he flipped his body around so that his striped paw stood on top of his wide head. The cat grinned wickedly.

Alice smiled. "Yes, actually!" She bent over backwards and brought her head down between her feet. She balanced on her right foot and placed her left foot on her head.

Hatter gasped and stared in amazement. The Cheshire Cat suddenly disappeared and reappeared in front of Alice. This time Hatter could see him. The Cat walked around Alice, his tail bristling in excitement and he said, "Wonderful! Fantastic!"

Alice had often played silly games like this as a child. Being a dancer and in gymnastics, she was very flexible and though she was small, she was strong. Alice slowly untwisted herself and stood up.

"Schrodinger." The Cheshire Cat slowly began to disappear starting with his tail and leading towards his head.

"Schrodinger! That is a funny name." She said watching him disappear one stripe at a time. "What does it mean?"

"That I am both here and not here. That I am two things at once that cannot coexist. I am in conflict with myself." The Cheshire Cat finally disappeared, his wide grin the last to go.

"But wait!" Alice cried. "Please! You must tell me how to get home. Can I get up the Rabbit Hole?"

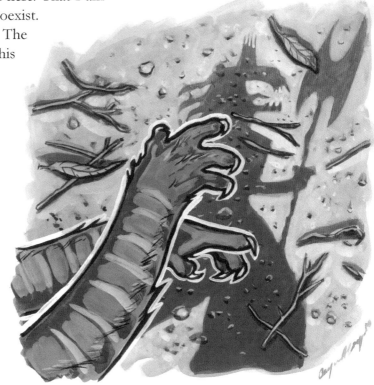

The cat appeared again, this time a different color and the stripes went the other way down his back.

"The Rabbit Hole is gone, destroyed. Not even the White Rabbit could help you now. Unless…" The Cat put its paws up to a ray of sunlight coming through the trees and on the ground a shadow appeared of the White Rabbit looking at his watch. "Unless it is re-made."

Then the shadow turned into the Queen of Hearts swinging an axe.

The Cheshire Cat laughed and said, "But he is difficult to get a hold of these days, isn't he?"

"Is he still alive?" Alice asked worried.

"Oh yes, he is still alive! The Queen doesn't yet have what she wants." He looked at Alice with bright yellow eyes.

"Is there any other way to leave Wonderland?" Alice asked. "Another Pool of Tears maybe?"

"The Pool of Tears is a one-way path into Wonderland. More tears would only get you wet. The only other way in or out that I know of is through the Looking Glass."

The cat made the shadow of a great mirror over a fireplace.

Hatter said, "But The Queen of Hearts said it was destroyed."

"The original Looking Glass was broken in two a long time ago. The Queen of Hearts took one half, the Red Queen kept the other. The larger half was brought to the castle of the Queen of Hearts, but soon after it was used to banish a would-be assassin..."

"Assassin!" Hatter shouted. "Preposterous!"

The Cheshire Cat ignored the outburst and continued showing the story by making shadow shapes on the ground. "Then the great Mirror was shattered. The Queen was so mad, magnificently mad, spectacularly mad! She managed to keep the largest shard however. But you know all about that, Alice."

"What?" Hatter asked.

Alice remembered the Queen had accused her of breaking her mirror. Did the Cheshire Cat think she did it too?

"How did the mirror break?" She asked.

The Cheshire Cat grinned. "I'll tell you if you can answer one question negatively."

Alice nodded.

"Tell me about your sister..."

Alice tightened her jaw. How could he know about her sister? She answered, "That is not a yes or no question."

"So nothing bad to say, eh?" The Cat flicked his tail.

Alice stomped on the last shadow that showed the Queen picking up a piece of glass. "So you're saying the only way I can get home is to rescue the White Rabbit from the Queen of Hearts or find this mirror shard? It's impossible!"

"And unlikely!" The Cat grinned.

"What about the other mirror? The Red Queen's mirror?" Alice asked.

"Oh, that was destroyed too. The Red Queen wants all portals destroyed and she started with her own Looking Glass. She went quite mad, in fact, and shattered every mirror in her castle." The Cheshire Cat grinned.

"I need to get back!" She cried.

"Why?" The Cheshire Cat asked in a sing-song voice.

"Because…. because my sister is dying," she revealed. "I don't have much time with her and I visit her every day. If I'm not there and she wakes or if she…" Alice had to stop. Hatter was silent.

"Getting home may not be so difficult, as long as you know the way. The Caterpillar will know."

Upon hearing the name Caterpillar, Hatter checked his pockets, then pulled out a tiny tea cup and took a sip.

"Where is the Caterpillar?" Alice asked.

"He runs a Book Shop in the garden near the White Queen's Castle." The Cat rolled over on his belly. "But is it really worth it? You could just stay here now that you're back and we could have so much fun! Accept your irrelevance. You cannot wage war on the Queen when you have nothing to wager."

"No one said anything about a war." Hatter said decidedly. "It's Tea Time, Alice, we should go now." Hatter took Alice by the arm and began walking away.

"But Time is all you need, isn't it?" The Cat said slyly.

Hatter turned around slowly. Up until now the Cat had not addressed him at all. Now his yellow eyes were focused on Hatter.

"Time is difficult to stop you know. He is in all places and all times happening together all at once. To draw him out, you need help. You need the White Rabbit's watch, you need the Queen's justice, and you need Alice, of course. Then Time will come."

Hatter stared at the Cheshire Cat.

"I am the bird and the worm. I am ever hunting me, and I fear I will devour myself." The Cheshire Cat narrowed his eyes at his own twitching tail, and leapt to catch it in his teeth. He was gone.

Alice turned to Hatter. "Really? That was ridiculous. Did we learn anything from him that would be helpful?"

"Yes," said Hatter calmly. "We need to get to the Caterpillar's Shop. And it's far off, on the other side of the Boardlands near the castle of the White Queen."

Alice wondered about what the Cat had said. Hatter needed *her* to summon Time? What did that mean?

Hatter walked quickly into the forest and called to Alice, "Hurry! We need to catch the train!"

"A train?" Alice asked, finding it strange that a train would exist here.

"Of course. The One-Away Train."

Chapter Eight: Ace in the Deck

Alice walked with Hatter through Ravenwood stopping only for a brief drink at a stream. A large eyed rainbow fish watched her curiously as she dipped her cupped hand in the cool water. She had not realized how thirsty she was and each sip of the stream seemed to make her even more thirsty.

"Alice, don't drink the water!" Hatter pulled her away muttering something about Silly Springs. Alice felt very refreshed. She skipped along humming to herself and laughing randomly. She stopped to watch the squirrels with the paint brush tails as they coated the trees in bright colors.

"Why do the squirrels paint the trees?" She asked. Picking up a paint flower, Alice tried to draw hearts on the trees but the paint disappeared after a few seconds.

"Why does the paint disappear so quickly?" She asked tossing the flower aside.

"Why do you always ask so many questions?" Hatter grinned.

"I do not always ask so many questions!" Alice twirled in a circle. "I just want to make some sense of this crazy place!"

"I think the Spring has affected you." He said as she clumsily leapt over a small fallen branch. "You're acting a bit…silly."

"Nonsense, it was only water." Alice skipped. "I'm just feeling a little less worried about things." She stepped into a soft patch of clovers and cartwheeled across without touching the ground, using her hands to press her dress down.

Hatter laughed and clapped as she curtsied.

"You really are a different sort of girl, aren't you? How did you stand on your head before? Even in a Wonderland that's a rare talent."

Alice smiled. "I have been in gymnastics as far back as I can remember. Competitions and practices took up all my after school hours. It's how I earned scholarships."

"So you've practiced

standing on your head, then?" He nearly laughed in his tea.

"Only for fun. And it was something none of the other girls could do." Alice twirled again.

"Did you ever wonder why you could do things no one else could?" He put his tea away.

"What do you mean?" She asked.

"I mean, did you ever feel that you didn't belong there. Like you were from somewhere else. Somewhere special."

"Hatter, I am not from Wonderland!" Alice felt her head spin and she had the urge to spin with it to catch up.

"But you must be! You shocked me with a touch, and then your tears brought you here. That could only have happened if you had been here before. Plus the Cheshire Cat even said that you were back!"

"No." Alice said. "You shocked *me*. It was your tears that brought us here and the Cheshire Cat never means what he says or makes any sense." Alice felt really fuzzy now.

Hatter continued, "Think about it. Have you ever fit in? Have you ever really felt at home on the Surfaceland?"

Alice stood in silence. He had hit upon her darkest fears and insecurities. She never really had a true home. Her family was not her own. Foster parents, gymnastics friends who were only ever in competition with her, and a boyfriend… ex-boyfriend, who never loved her. She had no future plans and no ambitions. But that didn't mean she was from this insane place. Why, she had grown up in London! She had a sister. A real sister that she loved. She put her hands on her head to try and stop the spinning. She wanted to think clearly.

"I have a sister." Alice said softly.

Hatter stepped closer to her, "Why didn't you tell me about her?" He asked. "You should have said she was the reason you needed to get back. Don't you have any other family to help?"

"No," she said softly, "My mother left us when we were young. I was six I think… and I remember she was also very sad and angry. Probably at our father, but I don't know, I never knew him. Lorina and I are alone."

"You have no other memories of your childhood?" His eyes flickered with light from within.

She closed her eyes and tried to remember, but she quickly opened them shaking her head, "Nothing, nothing more than dreams."

"Don't you see, Alice," Hatter stepped closer. "You are from here. This is where you belong."

"No, where my sister is, that is where I belong. And I need to get back to her. I'm asleep and this is a dream. I'll wake up any moment!"

"You can't still believe that. This is all real; I am real, see?" He pinched her on the arm and she quickly pulled away causing a new swirl in her head.

"I'm telling you the truth." He looked away slightly seeming to try and remember something. "And… I've seen you before… a long time ago…"

"What are you talking about?" Alice asked.

"What if I told you…that I knew you, but didn't know you?"

Alice slowly replied, "I'd say you're Mad."

Hatter stepped close to her suddenly, his eyes wild and he reached out for her shoulders.

He pulled her towards him and nearly nose to nose, he said, "We're all *mad* here."

Alice didn't pull away. She could smell the faint touch of earthy tea on his breath and his unblinking eyes seemed like an endless dark pool. She took in a sharp breath as he leaned even closer to her. She closed her eyes, her mind filling with a swirling jumble of desire, fear, and confusion.

A loud bang made Alice open her eyes and Hatter had turned his head away to look in the direction of the sound. He let Alice go and quickly pulled a bronze gun from his jacket pocket.

"What was that?" Alice asked recovering herself.

"With a blast like that, it must be the Red Queen's Bishops," muttered Hatter.

Another explosion rocked the wood. This time Alice could see swirling lights of color winding through the trees. One of the lights hit a tree and burnt a hole through it, shaking the tree so hard that its leaves fluttered to the ground catching fire as they fell.

Out of the woods, animals ran from the fires. Strange brightly colored birds ran on spindly legs while a group of green pigs cried out as they darted past. A giant stag raced by and shouted, "It's the Queen's Deck. Run!"

Hatter spun on his heel and grabbed Alice by the hand pulling her forward. He ran dragging her behind him, her feet barely touching the ground. Crackling lights whirled past them swirling like fireworks and smashing into trees with sparks flying. The trees caught fire as if made of dry tinder and the branches shook off their leaves sending flames cascading down like rain. Running through the falling fiery leaves, Alice felt her shoulder burn. She cried out and Hatter turned to her brushing the flaming leaf off her dress. He held out the strangely shaped gun and fired back; a purple shot of light blasted out and wound its way through the trees.

"Quickly, this way!" Hatter cried as a loud explosion nearly deafened them.

"How many are there?" Alice called as they ran.

"If it's a decacards, at least ten!" He pulled her through the trees firing back with his gun. She looked back at several white and red cards running through the trees surprisingly fast as they slipped through the narrowest of paths. One of Hatter's shots hit a card blasting it backwards into the air.

Hatter said, "Where did they get those guns? Must've stolen them from the Reds like I did." A blast came from in front of them and Hatter ducked as the sparks flew over, just missing his hat.

A Spade zipped through the trees impossibly fast holding his gun up towards Alice. She closed her eyes waiting for the shot, but Hatter grabbed the Spade around the neck threw him down flat onto the ground. Stepping on the Card's hand, he kicked the gun away, then placed his foot in the center of the card and folded it over so that it was bent in half. He let the Spade go and picked up the gun. As the card attempted to unfold itself, another three cards arrived.

"Take this!" Hatter tossed Alice the bronze gun that had many dials and knobs. A small glass vial attached to the gun held a thick purple liquid. Hatter aimed his gun at the center card and fired. The light beam hit the card blowing it backwards into a tree. The impact sent a shower of burning leaves down upon it setting the Suit on fire. Alice pointed her gun and

pulled the trigger. She nearly fell over as the blast shot just past one of the advancing cards.

The card on fire ran around in panicked circles until two other cards threw him to the ground and stamped out the flames. They turned towards Alice and aimed their guns directly at her. Alice braced herself this time, held the gun with both hands and fired.

Both cards blew backwards into the trees catching fire as they tangled in the branches. Hatter turned to her, grinned, and grabbed her hand pulling her again through the woods.

"I'm really sorry about this, Alice!" Hatter called as they ran. "I never thought the Queen would be this angry at me. I can't believe she would send her entire deck out here just to catch me!"

Alice said nothing. How could she explain to Hatter that Queen of Hearts was really after *her* for something she didn't do? Would he believe that she didn't have the watch; the one thing he wanted more than anything in the world? How could she admit that she was the reason his house was destroyed? Alice remained silent and ran on.

Hatter stopped and Alice almost ran into him. Through the trees she could see at least a dozen cards marching towards them. She turned around and saw even more cards coming up from behind.

"They've surrounded us!" She cried.

Hatter turned left and together they ran another minute dodging several blasts of colorful light. They stopped suddenly, blocked by a large fallen tree. Hatter lifted Alice onto the tree and jumped up climbing to the top. They stood back to back aiming their guns at the advancing cards. There were so many now Alice didn't know who to fire at or if it would make any difference.

Then a card came forward shoving the other cards out of the way. This card was different, larger, and it held a gigantic weapon over his shoulder. It was an Ace.

Ace moved forward and ordered the other cards to hold their fire.

"The Queen said, she wants 'um alive, and any Suit that causes harm to the target will deal with me!" The cards shuffled out of his way in fear.

"Ace!" Hatter called.

The card looked up at Hatter surprised. He called out, "Hatter, how did you get back?"

"Ace, come on, don't do this!" Hatter pointed his gun at the Ace whose weapon was ten times the size. "

"Sorry, Hatter. The Queens gave orders." Ace pointed the huge gun at Alice.

Hatter glanced behind him to see the surrounding cards closing in. "The Queens?" He asked, "You mean they are working together?"

"The Red Queen gave us these new weapons as part of some kind of deal. You cannot escape, so just put down the gun and come with us."

A dozen cards shuffled forward towards the fallen tree and Ace turned smashing one of the cards to the ground.

"I give the orders to move!" Ace yelled. "Stay back until I tell you!"

"But Ace," the Ten of Hearts argued, "The Queen's orders. We must capture…"

"I know the orders!" Ace smashed the Ten down and yelled at the others, "No one moves until I give the go ahead!"

Ace turned back to Hatter," Now what's going on, Hatter? What have you gotten mixed up in this time?"

"Ace, look," Hatter lowered his gun. "You know I had to come back, and I'm just helping a friend. Let us go."

"I can't help you this time. Both the Queens are together on the one and the Red Queen is dead serious.

Hatter looked behind him at the shuffling cards just waiting to attack. "What does the Queen want with me? Can she really still be upset?"

Ace looked confused for a moment, and then pointed his gun directly at Alice. "This isn't about you returning, Hatter. My orders are very specific, now give yourselves up."

"Ace, you owe me. Let us go."

"That was a long time ago, and you know I cannot defy the Queen. Besides, all I need is the g…"

A card from behind fired a shot and as Hatter and Alice ducked, Ace fired his gun over their heads and the massive blast hit the card instantly turning it to ash.

"I give the orders to fire!" Ace boomed. The cards shivered.

Hatter straightened hat as he stood up. He breathed out slowly.

"Alice," he said softly, "I'll give myself up, and you make a run for it. Once they have me, they won't follow you. Get to the train and find the Caterpillar. If I can get away I'll meet you there."

Hatter, no! Please, you can't leave me. I won't know where to go and you are my only friend here! If you give yourself up, so will I!"

Hatter stared at her for a moment, his eyes beginning to glow. "So you trust me?"

She wanted to tell him the truth but Ace fired the large gun blasting off one end of the fallen tree. The tree shook and Alice grabbed Hatter's hand as they struggled to keep their balance. One end of the dead tree caught fire.

"Come down, now!" Ace yelled. "And we won't have to make you."

Ace aimed the gun high and fired at the tree tops. The surrounding trees sparked and flaming leaves rained down. The dormouse peeked his head out for a moment then dove back into Hatter's pocket with a squeak. As the fire drew closer, Hatter aimed his gun at the shuffling deck and said, "I don't know how we're getting out of this one!"

To be continued...

Author Biography

Erin Pyne is a professional freelance writer in the Entertainment industry and trained dolphins for over 12 years in Orlando, Fl. Other works include the Red Angel series (2010), The Ultimate Guide to the Harry Potter Fandom (2010), and Dolphin Journey (2004). Her stories have been published in several anthologies and she has written articles in 'Art Nouveau Magazine' and 'The Ringlords News of Import'.

Erin has a B.A. in psychology from Rollins College and a Masters Certificate in conservation biology from the University of Central Florida. Erin studies martial arts, writes electronica music, and makes costumes in her spare time. She has an amazing son named Rowan William.

Follow Erin on Facebook, Twitter, and **ErinPyne.com**

Artist Biography

Cayce Moyer is a multi-media artist based out of Miami, Florida. She graduated from Savannah College of Art and Design in 2006 with a double BFA in Sequential Art and Painting and is now owner of her own freelance company SpaceCase Creations LLC. Projects range from book illustrations, sculptures, and sequential art to set and prop painting for live theater and television shows, conceptual design and more.

In her time off from working, Cayce enjoys playing sports, traveling, reading historical fiction, watching classic horror films and practicing homeopathic medicine through tea.

Follow Cayce Moyer on:
Facebook, Etsy, Deviant Art, GetArtworks, and LinkedIn to stay informed on future projects!

The story continues...

A
Curiouser and Curiouser
Series

Eat Me, Drink Me: Book Two

by Erin Pyne
and Cayce Moyer

Follow the Transformation at
www.Facebook.com/
CuriouserandCuriouserSeries.

Printed in Great Britain
by Amazon